RED, WHITE, & BAYOU

BADGES OF THE BAYOU

ERIN NICHOLAS

THE BADGES OF THE BAYOU SERIES

Gotta Be Bayou (Spencer & Max)
Bayou With Benefits (Michael & Ami)
Red, White & Bayou (Wyatt & Trudy)
Always Bayou (Beau & Becca)
Stuck Bayou (Theo & Savannah)

ABOUT THE BOOK

Wyatt Landry is back in town...for one night only. At least, that's the plan. In spite of the big Fourth of July party, and his cousin's plan to set him up with a friend of hers, and how much he wishes things could be the way they used to be.

But they're not. And he's hitting the road as soon as the sun sets

Until he sees her. The woman in the red dress. With the curves that make him think that he could stick around just a little longer...

Then she turns around, and *holy hell.*

Trudy Sinclair is back in town too. And she's all grown up.

Now he's face to face with the girl who was the reason for more than one of his broken bones, a few stitches, and his juvenile arrest record.

And the kiss he can't get out of his mind, even ten years later...

CHAPTER ONE

"WE'RE all going to head down to the bayou, sit in the truck beds to watch the fireworks, have some drinks, and camp out. It will be fun. You have to come with us."

And be the odd man out? He never spent the night in Autre anymore anyway, but since all of his cousins and now his brother were all coupled up, Wyatt had even more reason to head back to New Orleans when the sun started to go down.

"Nah, I'm just gonna head home." Wyatt gave his cousin's wife, Paige, a smile that was meant to convey that he was totally fine with this and that he was completely immune to her sweet smiles, puppy-dog eyes, and desire for everyone to be happy and included.

But Paige Landry was a very hard person to say no to. All of his cousins' wives were. His rowdy, trouble-making, always-up-for-a-good-time Landry cousins really had amazing taste in women it turned out.

He wasn't jealous. Much.

Would he like to find someone who completely understood him, made him a better man, kept him on his toes, and made him light up from inside the way his sister-in-law Max did to his brother Spencer?

Well, yeah. He wasn't an idiot.

But it was bullshit that these women could also work their charms on *him*.

"You can't leave before the fireworks," Paige said. "And then it will be late. Just stay. Camp out with us. We'll wake up and have breakfast tomorrow, and then you'll be here for the volley-ball tournament and all the fun!"

Dammit. That did sound fun.

Wyatt should have known better than to agree to come down here at all this weekend.

It was the fourth of July, and he was in the quaint, if slightly kooky, little town of Autre, Louisiana. The town held some of the best memories of his entire childhood, including this annual three-day event around Independence Day. He was surrounded by friends and family, great food, good music, and hard booze.

And he was probably going to be miserable.

He was always a little miserable in Autre. Now.

It hadn't been this way when he was growing up and spending summers here with his grandparents, running around with his brother and cousins, swimming, boating, fishing, being wild and rowdy, and getting dirty and ripping holes in every piece of clothing they owned. But it had been true for the past ten years or so.

His therapist, his best friend, and his brother, even his own conscience, thought it was time that he dealt with all of this.

But he'd been in town for three hours, eaten some great food, had a couple of beers, chatted with a bunch of old friends, seen most of his family...and he wanted nothing more than to get in his truck and head back to New Orleans.

Maybe he'd be able to stay next time.

"...she's funny, sweet, and fun," Paige was saying as he focused again on her argument for him staying tonight.

Wyatt groaned as his cousin's wife gave him a huge grin. "What? There's a girl?"

She laughed. "I know, it's *so* cruel of me to try to set you up this weekend with an amazing woman."

"I'm not looking for a date." Wyatt put his beer bottle to his lips and tipped it back.

Beer. That's what he was looking for. All he was looking for. Maybe something stronger.

"Okay, look, all of her friends and her sister are coupled up," Paige said. "She's been talking to this guy online, and he was supposed to come down and be her date this weekend, but he bailed at the last minute. Said they weren't 'to that point yet'. Whatever that means. She's sick of feeling like the third wheel. Or the fifth wheel." Paige gripped his arm. "She's not even going to come out to the fireworks because she doesn't want to be the only one there alone. *Please.*"

Yeah, something stronger, for sure. That was definitely what he needed. Because a little bit of him wanted to help this girl out. Depending on an online date for a big, multi-day event with friends and family was one thing, but having him back out at the last minute sucked.

Especially when the crowd you were spending the fourth of July weekend with was full of couples. Couples who had some big plan to turn their truck beds into cozy little romantic nooks to watch the fireworks from before spending the night.

"I'm supposed to camp out alone with some girl I just met?" he asked.

Paige grinned. "Well, we'll all be right there too, in our own trucks. But I'm not sorry that the only place to sleep is on a pile of pillows and blankets in the back of a truck under the stars next to a gorgeous girl. You poor thing. I'm so mean."

"It's not the only place," he told her. "I have a perfectly great bed back in New Orleans. And even if I didn't, I know the owners of about a dozen couches in this town."

Not that he'd use any of them. He'd waited to come down until after the parade, after the skits, after all the kids' games in the park. He'd shown up just in time to hang out with his family for a few hours at Ellie's bar—Ellie Landry was the grandmother to his favorite cousins and had married his grandpa's brother—partake in the crawfish boil, hear some live music, and then get back to New Orleans before the fireworks went off.

"It will be fun. No reason to worry," Paige went on, still squeezing his forearm where it rested on the arm of the lawn chair where he was lounging. "You're both single, and you'll be hanging out with all of us anyway. All you have to really do is hang out *beside* her."

"I hate setups," Wyatt told her. "And for an overnight campout? Come on. That's just asking for trouble. What if we can't stand each other after five minutes? Then we're stuck."

Paige laughed. "There's no way you won't be able to stand each other." She tipped her head. "You like *me*, don't you?"

Paige was awesome. She was sweet, kind, bright, fun, and gorgeous. Wyatt had absolutely no trouble understanding why his cousin Mitch had fallen head over heels for her in one night. She'd made Mitch work for it, but they were one of the best couples Wyatt knew.

But Wyatt studied Paige, pretending to have to think over his answer. "You're okay, I guess," he finally said.

She punched him in the bicep. "Well, she and I are really good friends. So you know you'll like her. I would never set you up with someone I thought you'd hate. And you are the only single guy I'd ever set *her* up with." She frowned. "I'm glad the online guy, Travis, isn't coming. He sounds like a dud."

Wyatt actually wasn't *completely* opposed to being set up. And he absolutely understood the feeling of being the odd man out.

The only reason he'd been back to Autre to visit in the past few years was to attend weddings, and we're-having-a-baby parties, and birthday parties for those babies.

His cousins on this branch of the family tree, and now even his brother, had all fallen in love and gotten married in the past few years. And as uncomfortable as he was in this sweet little town and as much as he'd avoided it for nearly ten years, he couldn't stay away from all their happiness completely.

So yeah, being the extra guy that made the group an odd number was familiar. It happened to him a lot around here—more and more all the time. And yeah, it did kind of suck.

Still, he hadn't spent the night here in over a decade.

"I don't know," he told Paige. "I'll think ab—"

"Oh, there she is!" Paige pointed at someone over his shoulder.

Wyatt turned to follow Paige's finger, but they were sitting on one the far side of the bonfire in front of Ellie's bar. The big crawfish boil was just getting cleaned up and the area was teeming with people. His eyes glanced over a woman in a red sundress with long, dark hair and then returned to her. He wasn't sure what it was about her, but he wondered who she was. "Which one?" he asked Paige.

"The red sundress. Dark hair. She's talking to Shelby."

Yep. He saw her. Okay, this was looking up.

She was facing away from them, but she was talking to a woman Wyatt knew well. He'd had a huge crush on Shelby Sinclair in high school. Well, she was Shelby Whitaker now. Had been for years. She'd married Scott, her high school sweetheart. The guy who'd been the reason Wyatt had never made an actual move on her.

Well, Scott, and Shelby's little sister, Trudy, who'd been the biggest cock-blocker of all time. It seemed any time Wyatt might have had a chance to spend some time with Shelby *without* Scott glued to her side, Trudy had been there or had needed something that pulled Wyatt away. He wasn't even sure if Shelby's younger, scrawny, talkative sister had been aware of what she'd been doing but…yeah, he was. Trudy had been sassy, mischievous, and full of trouble. And smart. Very smart. She'd known exactly what she was doing.

God, she'd irritated the hell out of him.

The woman in red bent over to retrieve a beer from the cooler at their feet, and Wyatt's gaze scanned over the delicious curve of her ass, and down her long, tanned legs. Suddenly the idea of sticking around Autre sounded a *little* better.

"Fine, you can introduce us," he said, finishing off his beer and pushing to his feet.

Paige's eyes lit up, and she scrambled to her feet. "Really?"

"Sure. No promises about staying, but I can at least meet her. See if she can make things a little more fun."

Paige paused, her brows pulling together in confusion. "You're not having fun?"

Right. Paige hadn't grown up here. She'd come to Louisiana only a couple of years ago. She might know that Wyatt and his brother Spencer hadn't grown up here but had spent every summer, holiday, and many long weekends in Autre when they were kids. She might know that there had been a huge explosion at the community center about ten years ago that had killed a bunch of people and injured several more. She might even know that Wyatt and Spencer's grandmother had been one of those killed.

But she might not know that Wyatt had been there that night. She definitely didn't know that he was supposed to stick around and help his grandmother clean up. That he'd told her he'd be right back.

And there was no way Paige knew that now, ten years later, he still had nightmares and survivor's guilt over all of that.

Wyatt took a deep breath and blew it out. "I've just been in a…weird mood. Autre just has a mix of memories for me."

Paige's frown deepened. "Oh. I'm sorry, Wyatt. I didn't know that."

Her husband, Wyatt's cousin Mitch, had been sitting quietly, listening. Now he spoke. "We're all worried about you, Wyatt."

Paige looked at him. "We are?"

He nodded. "We want you to start loving it here again," he said to Wyatt. "Like it used to be." He paused. "We miss you."

Wyatt blew out a breath. Mitch knew about his struggles. He and Mitch had always been close. Fuck. He didn't want everyone to worry about him. And…yeah, he missed them too. He knew he was missing out on some of the good times when he left early, or didn't come down at all.

Dammit.

He met Paige's gaze. "Well, maybe your friend can help me forget about some things and help me just focus on the fun."

Paige brightened at that, smiling and nodding. "She definitely can. She's *a lot* of fun. Everyone thinks so. We have such a good time together."

Wyatt looked at Mitch. The other man nodded encouragingly.

Well, that was definitely what he needed. A lot of fun. A good time. What the hell? Might as well try it with a curvy brunette who Paige clearly adored.

They crossed the grass toward Shelby and Paige's friend. Wyatt studied Shelby as they got closer. She was still beautiful. She looked almost exactly the way she had in high school. Long blonde hair, sparkling green eyes, slender body, a fashionable sundress, sandals that wrapped around trim ankles with perfectly painted toenails. Shelby had always been put together, and pretty.

But now he just felt…nostalgic, he supposed…about seeing her. There was no rush of emotion of any kind, really. Not desire, not affection. He hadn't known her well enough, really, to feel affectionate toward her. Then or now. Shelby was objectively beautiful, and he supposed if they were both single and met up in a bar and started flirting, if she showed any interest, he'd be attracted to her. But that desire to impress her and get closer to her that he'd felt in high school was completely gone.

Huh.

On the contrary, when the brunette turned at Paige's greeting and he met her gaze, and he registered who he was looking at, he felt a *huge* rush of emotions.

Shock. Frustration. Holy-shit-I've-missed-her. And desire. Impossible-to-miss-desire. Which just made his frustration stronger.

She'd gotten taller. And curvier. But Trudy Sinclair looked up at him with wide brown eyes that he'd know anywhere.

CHAPTER TWO

Well… great.

She was going to be sharing her truck bed for the fireworks with the guy she'd been in love with for most of her teenage years.

Really, that *should be* great, right?

Sure.

Except, he was also the guy who hated her.

Yeah…great.

And, to make things even *more* fucking great…Wyatt Landry had grown up. Very, very nicely.

Muscles, tattoos, great scruff…

Just. Fucking. Great.

Shelby greeted him with a bright, sweet smile. "Wyatt! Oh my gosh! It's great to see you!"

See? *Great.*

And her sister's sweetness was irritating as hell.

Everything Shelby did was sweet and had been from, literally, the day she'd been born. Their parents loved to tell about what a great baby Shelby had been while Trudy had been colicky and cranky. Trudy was used to Shelby's sweetness. It was genuine. It was hard to be annoyed with someone who was authentically kind and warm, even if, just every once in awhile, it would be nice if that person got riled up and shouted, or made a mistake, or called someone a bitch when they were being a bitch.

But no. Shelby never did any of that. That was just who she was. So why did her smiling sweetly, as she *always* did, at Wyatt rub Trudy the wrong way right now?

"Hey, Shelby."

Oh, his voice had gotten deeper too.

Great.

Maybe, just maybe, Trudy thought, she was extra annoyed because when *he* looked at Shelby he smiled too.

God, she'd always loved his smile.

"You guys already know each other?" Paige asked, looking back and forth between all of them.

"Of course we do," Shelby said with a light, pretty laugh. "Wyatt's the best. We've missed seeing you," she said to him.

They'd missed seeing him? Trudy frowned. Her sister and her brother-in-law didn't live in Autre anymore, but they were here with their kids visiting their parents a lot. Like, *a lot*.

Wyatt had been a typical Landry boy in every way. A carefree, laid-back, flirtatious playboy. He'd loved boating, swimming, fishing, bonfires, staying out late, talking, laughing, and partying. She knew for a fact that his summers in Autre were some of the best times of his life. Up until the death of his grandmother.

"It's been awhile," Wyatt agreed.

It had? Trudy had been *very* good about not asking about Wyatt, but she didn't know that Shelby and Scott hadn't seen him in 'awhile'. What did that mean? And why? What had he been up to? Did he still live in New Orleans? The last she'd known, he'd gone into the Coast Guard.

Now she was dying to know all about him.

Great.

"That's amazing," Paige said, clearly delighted by the news they were all being reunited. "Mitch didn't say anything about you already knowing each other. But that makes sense, I guess."

Trudy almost laughed at that. If Mitch hadn't mentioned the little detail of Wyatt not only *knowing* Trudy, but also that she was the absolute last person he'd even want to see, not to mention cuddle up with for fireworks, then Mitch had a reason. Mitch must be trying to get back at Wyatt for something.

Because Trudy had been annoying Wyatt Landry for as long as she could remember.

She didn't think, even all these years later, that Wyatt had told anyone *all* of the stuff he'd gotten into because of her. But the blood had been hard to hide. And he'd needed to call for backup a couple of times. That backup had been Mitch. Unless they needed an actual adult, then they'd called his cousin Sawyer. That had only happened once, but that had *not* been fun.

She couldn't help but focus on the little bump on the bridge of his nose where he'd broken it. Twice. Because of her.

And she knew for a fact that he had a huge scar on the palm of his left hand. Because of her.

And he had a juvenile arrest record. Because of her.

That was the time they'd had to call Sawyer.

And those were just the permanent things. There were lots of other instances where she'd dragged him into a circumstance where things had gone badly for him. Because of her.

And who could forget the last time she'd ever seen him? The night he'd found out she had feelings for him. The night they'd kissed. The night his grandma had been killed in the huge explosion at the community center.

Oh yeah, they definitely knew each other.

"We do." Trudy finally spoke, turning to one of her best friends with a smile when Wyatt said nothing.

He was too busy staring at her.

"Wyatt and Spencer used to come down here in the summers and on holidays," Trudy explained. "We've known each other since we were kids."

"Oh my gosh!" Paige looked excited now.

Crap.

"That's amazing!" Paige gushed. "This will be perfect! You can hang out and catch up and you won't have to do that awkward getting-to-know-you stuff. You can just jump right in."

Trudy wasn't sure what Paige thought they were going to jump right in to, but...well, they definitely didn't need to get to know each other. Wyatt knew some stuff about her that no one else did.

And she'd love to know more about him.

Because she was stupid and had never fully gotten over her crush on him, apparently.

Great.

She hadn't thought of Wyatt Landry in a long time.

Much.

Okay, since moving back to Autre in January, she'd thought of him more because...well, how could she not? He'd been her first love—even unrequited love counted—and everywhere she went in Autre had memories that involved him.

And he wasn't the only one who had broken bones and scars from some of the times they'd spent together.

But during the years she'd lived in Colorado, she really hadn't thought of him much. Honestly.

She did know that he didn't come to Autre for holidays anymore and that had worked out nicely for her. She hadn't accidentally run into him downtown at Christmas time, or around town while trick-or-treating with her niece and nephew, or in the park on the Fourth of July...until now.

She met his gaze directly. "Um, actually," she said in response to Paige's comment. "That's probably not a good idea."

She should have said no to the whole couples' camping thing from the beginning. Taking Travis to that would have been awkward too. She'd already felt like things weren't going to go anywhere with the guy and her relief when he'd cancelled had been a pretty good validation of that. But *God* she hated being the only person not in a couple when she hung out with her sister and friends.

It used to be fine. There used to be other single people, and Shelby and Scott had been ShelbyandScott—said as one word and thought of as one person—for so long that they almost didn't feel like a couple. But now *everyone* in her family and friend group was paired up. The feelings of being left out gave her flashbacks to high school when their mom and dad made Shelby take Trudy everywhere she went.

That rule had been multi-faceted. It had been designed to keep both girls out of trouble. Shelby was supposed to keep Trudy's wild-child tendencies in check, while Trudy was supposed to act as a sort-of deterrent to Shelby and Scott becoming teen parents. Essentially they were forced to hang out together. Which they did.

But they also made deals.

Trudy went out with them… then could go do whatever she wanted while Scott and Shelby did whatever *they* wanted. Then the girls would meet up again to go home, or to show up at home at the same time.

But, Shelby also got on birth control, unbeknownst to their mother, *and* they used condoms all the time, and Trudy had a list of people she could call to bail her out of trouble.

Over time, that list had been narrowed down a lot. To one person. Wyatt.

But that was his own fault. He'd started showing up all on his own. She hadn't actually started calling him until after he'd proven to be reliable, and good at everything, and a fantastic secret keeper.

Well, and until after she'd realized he had a crush on Shelby. Then Trudy started calling him to keep him away from Shelby.

Teenage guys were so stupid.

And easily manipulated.

"Why not?" Paige asked, her expression full of disappointment. "You'll both be hanging out with us all anyway, right?"

"I just think Wyatt would be more comfortable if he wasn't forced to hang out with *me*," Trudy said, not looking at Wyatt.

"Oh," Paige said, understanding dawning. "Do you guys not get along?" She looked from Trudy to Wyatt and back with a wince. She looked up at Mitch. "Why didn't you tell me that."

"I didn't—" Mitch started.

"It's not Mitch's fault," Trudy jumped in quickly. She still wasn't looking at Wyatt but she could feel his eyes on her. "It's just been a long time and…it's complicated."

It wasn't. Wyatt hated her. It was pretty simple. But she didn't want to go into what had happened that last night they'd been together.

Paige's eyes rounded and, dammit, now she looked curious and Trudy knew she was going to have to fill Paige in. Dammit.

"Did you guys date in high school?" Paige asked, looking *very* interested. It was clear she wanted that answer to be yes.

Trudy shook her head quickly. "No. God, no. Absolutely not. It's not that. It's definitely not that. No. Nope. *Definitely* not."

Paige's eyes were now wide, but for a different reason.

Trudy was pretty sure the Shakespeare quote about the lady protesting too much was running through Paige's head right now.

Paige's mouth opened to reply, but Trudy felt a big, hot hand wrap around her upper arm—her *bare* upper arm—and a deep voice say, "Can I talk to you?"

Wyatt did not wait for her to answer his obviously-not-really-a-question. He started across the grass, dragging her with him.

Upper arms were not erogenous zones. But Trudy's body decided to rebel and make it into one. Tingles were spreading through her body from where he held her in a firm grasp, that didn't hurt, but that she absolutely was not getting out of.

"Hey!" She tugged on her arm.

He didn't let go until they were behind the big wooden stand that was selling frozen lemonade and kettle corn.

He pushed her up against the surprisingly solid structure, braced his hands on either side of her head, and leaned in, his gaze direct.

"What. The. Fuck. Trudy?"

CHAPTER THREE

Damn him.

They hadn't stood this close to one another very often. Certainly not since that time they'd kissed. Of course, that had also been the last time she'd seen him until now.

And the fact that she still remembered that kiss ten years later, thought about it when other guys kissed her, thought about the way he'd groaned, slid his fingers into her hair, holding her still as he'd opened his mouth to deepen the kiss, then ran his hands down her back to cup her ass and squeeze before picking her up and turning to put her up against the side of his truck, drove her nuts.

Of course, there was also the time she'd fallen on him when they'd been trying to push her car out of the ditch. They'd been pretty close that night. Or the time she'd fallen on him when he'd been boosting her up to try to save a nest of baby squirrels that had been abandoned when their mother had been hit by a truck. Or the time he'd been trying to boost her up so she could sneak in through her bedroom window after curfew.

Yeah, they'd been close a few times (and he'd touched her ass a few times). But not like this. Not with him staring at her with this intensity. Not with all the history between them. Not with him knowing she'd been in love with him. Not since he'd started hating her.

Now whenever she smelled kettle corn or tasted frozen lemonade, she would think of him.

So yeah, damn him. Because she really liked both of those things and she didn't need to be thinking about freaking Wyatt Landry for the rest of her life whenever she smelled them.

"What the fuck *what*?" she snapped, irritated.

"Hanging out together is a bad idea? I wouldn't be comfortable? Things are complicated?"

"Things *are* complicated. It *is* a bad idea." Trudy wanted to push him back, but she was afraid to touch him.

Afraid she'd want to keep touching him. Afraid she'd accidentally pull him closer instead of pushing him away.

He lifted a brow in a very cocky expression. "I thought you were in love with me. That was what you were tellin' people the last time we saw each other."

The jerk was just going to put that out there like that? Trudy narrowed her eyes. "You and I both know I said that just so Shelby wouldn't go out with you. And that was *ten years ago*."

He nodded slowly, his gaze dropping to her lips.

Her lips liked that.

Her head, that knew she was not really over this guy, did *not*.

"Yeah, you *really* didn't want me to date your sister."

"No, I really didn't."

His gaze came back to hers. "Because you wanted me for yourself."

Trudy rolled her eyes. Yes. But the ego on this guy had only grown it seemed. Along with his muscles. And the number of tattoos he had.

She forced herself to act unaffected. "Because everyone knew that Scott and Shelby belonged together. Because he was her soulmate. Because they had been broken up for about three hours when you decided to go after her. We all knew they were gonna get back together. I didn't want her doing anything that she would regret or that might mess up them getting back together. Or that would—"

She stopped before she blurted the rest of that thought out. It had been about her *sister*. And that other guy. Fuck, what was his name? Scott. Yes, Scott. Her brother-in-law.

But dammit, when Wyatt was standing this close, it was hard to think of other men. Not to mention details about them, like their names.

Wyatt frowned, but his gaze dropped to her lips again. She felt heat shoot through her and settle low between her legs. Dammit.

"Or that would what?" he asked. His voice was huskier.

Well, she'd come this far. "Break *your* heart."

Surprise flickered in his gaze as it returned to hers. "You were thinking about me?"

"Of course." She frowned. "We were friends. I didn't want *anyone* to get hurt."

"Huh," he said. "That all sounds really good," he agreed.

But Trudy had the impression that he didn't fully buy it.

Fine. Whatever. That was all actually the truth about why she'd chosen to tell her sister how she felt about Wyatt *that* night.

But *what* she'd told Shelby had been real and true for a long time before that. She *had* been in love with Wyatt.

"Seems everything worked out for them, didn't it?" he asked.

Trudy lifted her chin and met his gaze. "It definitely did. So I was right."

"But what about you?" His eyes narrowed. "What are you doin' here single? Online dating?"

"What do you mean?"

"You left town, changed your number, your sister and Scott moved, I didn't know how to get ahold of you. Next thing I knew you were engaged."

Trudy stared at him. He'd known about Ben?

"I…was…" I nod stupidly. "I went to college and got a new number. Scott and Shelby moved too."

He moved one hand off the wall next to her head and cupped her cheek. "I thought you were married, Tru."

Tru.

Not many people called her Tru. It was a nickname saved for especially affectionate moments with very special people.

But Wyatt had called her Tru. And then True Blue one night when they were sixteen, and he'd been the one to call *her* for help. He'd had too much to drink and had needed a ride, and she'd shown up without question. He'd been drunk, but he'd remembered the nickname. He'd kept using it and had shortened it to Blue.

He was the only one who called her that.

Trudy wet her lips. "No. I…broke it off."

"Oh." He studied her face, brushing his thumb over her cheek almost absent-mindedly. "Sorry to hear that."

"You are?" she asked without thinking.

"No. Not even a little bit."

And holy shit, she forgot how to breathe.

A few seconds passed of them just staring at each other. Trudy didn't know about him, but she sure as hell was replaying their one and only kiss.

It was the kiss she still compared all other kisses to.

He'd been seventeen. Yes, Wyatt Landry—like all the Landry boys—had kissed his fair share of girls by then, but still…how much better could he be at it now?

"How about this guy who was supposed to meet you this weekend?" Wyatt asked, his voice gruffer now.

"I don't think it's going to work out."

"I'm not sorry to hear that either."

She let one corner of her mouth curl up.

"Seems you need me to bail you out of a problem again," he said thoughtfully.

"What do you mean?"

"Every time I was here, there was something you needed from me. Now here we are again," he said. "You need a date.

Someone to keep you from being a…." He paused and seemed to be adding something up. "Ninth wheel out there on the bayou tonight."

Oh…really?

Well, she *would* be the ninth person if she went along with her sister, Scott, Paige, Mitch, and the two other couples tonight. Which she would *not* do. Not alone anyway.

"You're single too," she pointed out. "And having your cousin's wife find *you* a date."

He gave her a little grin, and she felt her belly swoop. "That was all Paige's idea."

"You didn't want to be set up?"

"Not until I saw you bend over to get a beer out of the cooler."

Yeah, her belly liked that too. It gave another swoop. And a part a little lower tingled too.

"Is that right?"

"Yep. Didn't even know who you were. Imagine my delight when I realized that the woman in the red sundress with the amazing ass and great legs was none other than the girl who was madly in love with me and kissed me like I was a strawberry beignet dipped in chocolate sauce."

Trudy's mouth dropped open.

First, he thought her ass was amazing?

Second, those beignets—and her unabashed love for them— were a secret!

That was one of those things he knew about that no one else did.

There was a café in New Orleans that made specialty beignets that her family was forbidden to go to because her grandmother's best friend from high school ran it, and they were definitely not best friends anymore. In fact, they were sworn enemies. But also because, according to Trudy's grandmother, beignets were *not* supposed to be filled and were *only* to be covered in powdered sugar. What her ex-best friend-now-mortal-enemy was doing to beignets was a travesty. Her grand-mother's words, not Trudy's.

But Trudy went to the café regularly because the beignets were *to die for*. When she did, she used an alias and wore a cap and fake glasses. And she had once, with Wyatt as the only witness, polished off a plate of strawberry beignets dipped in dark chocolate sauce and then literally licked the bowl of choco-late sauce clean.

He'd promised never to tell anyone that she was having an affair with beignets that were not made by her grandmother. Or that she was an absolute pig about it.

"I did *not* kiss you like that," she finally said. "And actually, I believe *you* kissed *me*."

He leaned in until their noses were almost touching. "I did. You're right. But you most definitely kissed me back, Tru." He paused. "Like I was a fucking beignet filled with all your favorite things."

Okay, yeah, she had.

"And you're the one who told everyone you were in love with me," he added, leaning back again. But looking *very* smug.

Why did he keep bringing that up?

"I told *Shelby*," Trudy said. "To keep her from going out with you," she added.

But Wyatt gave her a knowing look. "You still said it. And she told me. And you did *not* deny it when I asked you."

"I couldn't deny it. Your tongue was in my mouth!"

Instead of laughing or arguing that point, Wyatt's gaze seemed to heat. "Yeah, it sure was."

Oh wow, it was definitely hot out here.

"So now you're just fine with being set up?" she asked. "You're going to be the tenth wheel out there with me?"

"Oh, it has to be me," he said. "I mean, when you have a problem in Autre, I'm the one who takes care of you, right, Tru?"

Damn, that idea of him taking care of her made her mind go skittering off in all kinds of dirty directions.

Trudy didn't know if being without a date tonight for the fireworks was a *problem*, but…yeah, Wyatt always took care of her. And dammit, this chemistry was real. If he wanted to play it off as him doing her some kind of 'favor' like he'd done when they were kids, fine, she could go along with that. It meant she'd get to spend more time with him.

Maybe she'd even get to apologize.

Or at least, make a new *good*, fun memory with him in this town that would help to heal that last time they'd been together.

She nodded. "You were always my first call, Wyatt."

Something flickered in his gaze. "I'll just put tonight on your tab." He dragged his thumb back and forth along her jaw. "But one of these days, I'm going to collect, Blue."

Oh, yeah, that wasn't her stomach feeling flutters when he called her Blue and talked about collecting on her tab in that rough tone of voice.

What was happening?

"My…" She had to clear her throat. "…tab?"

It occurred to her that she wasn't noticing the smell of kettle corn and lemons. Everything around her was Wyatt. All she could see were his piercing green eyes. All she could feel was the heat of his body and the tingles in *her* body that being this close to him elicited.

And all she could smell was him. He wore a cologne that was crisp and fresh and made her want to bury her nose against his neck. But he also had a scent that was just him, a combination of his shampoo and laundry detergent and soap and being outdoors and just him.

Which elicited an urge to run her nose and lips all over his body and not just his neck.

"Oh yeah. You have a running tab with me. All the times I was there for you."

"I didn't realize you were keeping track."

Did he really remember all the times they'd spent together?

That was kind of sweet. *She* definitely remembered all the times he'd shown up and been her hero.

"Well, let's see," Wyatt said. "I've had my nose broken, once when you fell on me, and once when I confronted a guy who was harassing you at a party. I have a huge scar on my palm from trying to haul your car out of the ditch. I broke my wrist falling off a roof, trying to keep *you* from falling off that roof."

Oh, well, sure, if he was going to just remember the bad times when he ended up being permanently marred by the ordeal. Those were probably easier to keep track of.

And that wasn't exactly sweet.

He went on. "I missed playing in our championship baseball game because your car broke down two hours from here, and you needed someone to come get you. I missed my brother's epic eighteenth birthday party, which people still talk about because you needed a ride to the hospital—"

"Hey!" Trudy broke in. "It was an acute appendicitis. I could've died if someone didn't take me. That was hardly my fault."

He narrowed his eyes to silence her and continued. "I spent the night in the county jail and have a permanent mark on my record because you told me that you needed help getting something back from a guy, but you didn't tell me that his father, who caught us trying to pry open a back window on his house was a county deputy and would press charges for breaking and entering, and trespassing. And… am I forgetting anything? Oh yes, you cock blocked me constantly with the woman of my dreams."

Trudy snorted at that. "You and Shelby were never meant to be. I might apologize for the other things—except the appendicitis—but not for that one. Never for that one."

He leaned in until their noses were almost touching again and dropped his voice to a low growl, "But you admit to being a cock blocker."

She tried to hide the fact that she was suddenly breathless. "Absolutely."

He studied her, still caging her in.

Her heart was already beating fast, but now, for some reason, it kicked into an even higher cadence.

"Yeah, I think it's time to collect."

Her eyes widened, and she started to protest, but then she thought about it. She did kind of have a 'tab' with him. She'd been a troublemaker, and Wyatt had been there for her several times, over and over. It wasn't exactly her fault that he had broken bones and scars and other trouble, but…it kind of was. All of those instances had been things she'd instigated. Except, again, the appendicitis. But she'd told him to call her mom or her sister, and he'd refused.

She still remembered how scared he'd looked as he'd carried her to his car and then driven like a bat out of hell to the hospital. The way he'd stayed by her bed in the emergency room, never letting go of her hand, and how they'd had to peel him away from her to take her for the scans to determine what was causing her symptoms.

He'd been the first face she'd seen when she woke up from the emergency appendectomy. Her family had been there by then. He hadn't had to stay.

But he did.

Right there by her bed.

That was the night she'd been sure she was in love with Wyatt Landry.

She thought about that a lot. Too much. It was annoying as fuck.

But now, there was something in his eyes, heat, interest…*something* that made her ask, "So what do I owe you?"

"You're gonna pay up?"

She lifted a brow. "That makes it sound serious."

He held up his hand, the one that had been cupping her face, opening his palm. The scar was still there, still very visible and big. She'd forgotten how it had sliced all the way from the base of his pinky across his hand to the base of his thumb.

"Okay, fine. What do you want?" she asked.

"Help me get through this weekend."

She was surprised. "What do you mean?"

"It's…tough for me to be here in Autre for long periods. I come and go quickly usually. But my friends and family want me to stick around this weekend." He stopped and studied her face. "I didn't think I could do it, but then…I saw you. Now I'm thinking I might have a chance."

Trudy had trouble pulling in a full breath. Wow. This was not at all what she'd expected when she'd come to the crawfish boil, or when Paige had said *I want to introduce you to someone*, or even when she'd first seen Wyatt.

But Wyatt Landry—her long-time crush, the guy she'd last seen on a *horrible* night ten years ago, the guy who had always been there for her, and, most importantly, someone she considered a *friend*—thought she could help him through something tough this weekend?

She was in.

She immediately wanted to say a blanket, *yes, whatever you want.* Instead, she took a breath and asked, "How can I help?"

"Well, like this, for starters." His hand was back on her face, but now he tipped her head back slightly as he leaned in.

Then he kissed her.

She gasped.

Oh, *great.*

But seriously…this was *great.* Amazing. Fantastic.

Their first kiss had been toe-curling.

Getting a face-cupped French kiss from the boy you've crushed on for two years? A dream come true.

But Wyatt Landry was now a man. With ten years of kissing experience.

Now Wyatt *owned* her mouth. His hand moved from the back of her head to cup her chin, his thumb pressing gently but firmly, opening her mouth and then licking over her lower lip, then inside to tangle his tongue with hers. His other hand dropped from the wall to her lower back, bringing her closer, pressing her against his body. His big, hard, *hot* body.

She moaned and wrapped her arms around his neck, lifting on tiptoe to get closer. His hand left her back to slide down and squeeze her ass, and then she noticed the big, hard bulge behind his fly.

Ohmygod. Wow. *Yes.* Wyatt Landry was turned on. By her. By this kiss.

She pulled back, stunned. Delighted. Stunned. Wondering if she was dreaming. And stunned. Had she hit her head?

He was breathing hard as he stared back. And he hadn't removed his hands from her body.

She swallowed.

He nodded. "Yeah. I think this is a great plan."

This plan was…stunning.

But…

Now she looked at *his* mouth.

Holy. Crap.

Yeah. This was a really great plan, actually.

He finally moved his hand off of her butt, and she sank back down onto her flat feet.

"So…we're just going to…hang out?"

He lifted a hand and tucked a strand of her hair behind her ear. "Yeah. I guess all you have to do is be yourself, Tru. God knows you always were distracting, and I hardly ever had time to think about anything else when I was with you. Seems that hasn't changed."

Her heart definitely flipped at that and started racing.

But dammit. Her brain was also going a mile a minute.

She'd distracted him that last night they'd been together. He'd come to find her instead of being with his grandmother. He'd been at the community center with Ruth, helping her clean up after the big picnic and auction. But he'd left her to come find Trudy after Shelby had told him Trudy was in love with him.

He'd been with her instead of his grandmother.

If he'd been with Ruth, maybe she wouldn't have been inside the community center. Maybe she would have already left. Maybe she wouldn't have died that night.

Trudy had been dealing with her guilt over that night for ten years. Her therapist and her friends had assured her it wasn't her fault. She knew that, on some level.

But she knew Wyatt also had to think about how he'd been with her instead of his grandmother. She hated the idea that he might blame her.

She'd always been trouble for Wyatt.

There was no denying that she'd gotten into a lot of messes. And sure, when they were trying to push cars out of ditches, sneaking around someone's house trying to steal his favorite signed baseball, or rescuing baby animals, it was probably hard to focus on anything else in the moment.

"So you want to get a swamp boat stuck somewhere? Or steal something? I don't have another appendix, but I've still got my gall bladder. I could work on doing something to get that removed, I guess."

He ran a hand from her ear down her neck, over her shoulder, and down her arm to link their fingers.

Despite all of her thoughts about being a problem for him, she still felt a shiver of *God, I want him to keep touching me like that.*

"I think it can be simpler than that," he said. "Just don't leave my side, and make sure I have a hell of a good time."

Trudy swallowed. A good time could mean so many different things. Her brain was screaming, *this is a really bad idea. This is a really bad idea. You're really gonna regret this. He's gonna break your heart. Your sixteen-year-old heart and your twenty-six-year-old heart.*

But the rest of her body was yelling, *but it might mean more kissing or even more than that! Dream come true. Live in the moment! You can deal with the fallout later.*

She was under no delusion that Wyatt Landry was going to fall madly in love with her, and that they were going to live happily ever after like Shelby and Scott.

But this guy had been her crush for years. She felt *terrible* about the last time they'd seen each other. And for a chance to spend one weekend with him, being his date, sticking right by his side no matter what, helping him make some good memories, *kissing him some more*?

She met his gaze, and a slow smile curled his lips as he nodded.

"Say yes, Tru."

Well, she'd always been a risk taker. The idea that she might get into trouble had never deterred her from the next wild—and probably terrible—idea.

"Yes."

CHAPTER FOUR

Damn this was a good idea.

He was on his back in the bed of Trudy Sinclair's truck, on a pile of blankets and pillow, just as Paige had described.

Trudy had three solar-powered lanterns set up that cast a soft glow around them and a little fan that blew a natural bug repellent that smelled like vanilla around them.

The sound of the bayou gurgling by, the frogs and crickets singing their night songs, and their friends talking and laughing softly from their own truck beds, filled the air. The sky was a deep orange with streaks of purple and pink in the west, and the deep blue of the night was slowly creeping in.

It was the perfect sky for fireworks.

He and Trudy lay side-by-side looking up, not speaking, at least six inches of space between them.

And Wyatt hadn't been this content in a very long time. Anywhere, but especially not in Autre, Louisiana.

He was feeling a million times better about…well, everything. He'd always wanted to want to stay in Autre. He wanted to participate in all the activities with enthusiasm and happiness, with no cloud hanging over his head. He wanted to see the fireworks, and camp out by the bayou, and wake up here tomorrow, ready for even more fun and celebration. Things he hadn't done in over a decade.

And now he had the perfect way to make that happen.

Trudy Sinclair.

If he needed a distraction, this girl was *it*. There was no better word to describe her as a matter of fact.

There wasn't a single time he could remember being with Trudy when his entire focus hadn't been fully on *her*.

And she owed him.

He had been there for her, pulled her sweet ass out of trouble, covered for her, *lied* for her, fucking gone into battle for her.

And now, the idea of spending the next twenty-four hours with her plastered to his side was the best fucking thing he'd thought up in a long time.

Who would have thought that the annoying little trouble-maker would turn into a sexy woman who smelled like sunshine, felt like heaven, sounded like an angel when she sighed against his lips, but kissed like a little devil?

You did, you dumbass. You thought all of that. A few times. Don't pretend you're shocked.

He told his inner voice to shut up.

He'd pushed the memory of hearing that Trudy loved him and their kiss to the very back of his mind.

But if the explosion hadn't happened at that exact same moment… Maybe if that wasn't the night your grandmother died. Maybe if that wasn't the beginning of all the horrible shit and had just been another summer night in Autre…

Okay *now* he shut those thoughts down.

It didn't matter. It didn't matter what might have been or what might have happened if that hadn't been the worst night of his life. Because it had been. He'd left Autre the next morning and nothing had ever been the same.

"You okay?" Trudy asked softly.

He looked over at her. He took a deep breath. He realized that he'd been getting tense, thinking about that night. "Yeah."

"You were tensing up."

He smiled at her. He liked that she'd been paying attention to him. "Sorry. Was just thinking about…some things."

She rolled to her side to face him. "What things? You don't have to talk about it, but if you want to, you can."

He nodded. "My grandma."

She sucked in a quick breath. "Oh."

"Yeah. It's been…hard to come back here since that night. I feel…" He blew out a breath. But he realized it shouldn't feel weird to confess something to Trudy. They'd kept a lot of secrets for one another and she'd been there that night. She knew what had happened. Or, at least, most of it. He didn't have to spell it all out. "Guilty."

Her eyes widened. "Why do you feel guilty?"

"Because I wasn't there."

She winces and rolls back to her back. "Yeah. But that's not your fault."

He'd been told that over and over. By his friends, his brother, his parents, and his therapist. He knew it. Basically. He knew his grandmother wouldn't have blamed him for doing what he did that night. But…it didn't change that he hadn't been there for her. With her.

But he hadn't been with her because of the woman lying next to him right now.

"It's mine."

At first Wyatt wasn't sure he'd heard the words correctly. Then he wasn't sure the words had come from Trudy. Maybe they'd come from one of the other truck bed, part of another, unrelated conversation.

But in the fading light he could see she was pressing her lips together and now she was the one holding herself very tense.

"What?"

She didn't answer. He scooted closer to her and put a hand on her arm. She flinched slightly.

"Trudy. Look at me." He kept his voice low, not wanting anyone else to overhear.

She swallowed and slowly rolled her head so she was facing him.

"What are you talking about?" he asked.

"It's my fault you weren't there," she said softly. "And I don't blame you for hating me for it. But I'm so sorry. I've felt terrible about it ever since."

He frowned. She thought it was *her* fault? She was definitely the reason he'd left the community center, but…

He blew out a breath and reached out, taking her hand, and lacing their fingers together. "Jesus, Tru, I never blamed you for it. I blamed myself, my emotions, my hormones…timing, fate, bad luck…anything I could think of. But it wasn't anyone's fault. Not mine. Definitely not yours."

Trudy sighed. "I mean, yeah, okay, technically. But if I hadn't been so jealous of Shelby, or if I hadn't been such a chicken, or if I had just accepted we were just friends…"

Suddenly Wyatt rolled until he was braced on one elbow beside her, nearly on top of her. "What are you saying? Chicken about what? Just friends? We weren't just friends."

Her eyes were wide as she stared up at him. "I mean if I'd just kept my mouth shut and never said anyth—"

"*No*," he cut her off, frowning. "I'm glad you finally said something." He thought about what he'd just said.

Yes, he meant it.

Finding out Trudy had feelings for him that were more than friendship had rocked his world. So much so that he'd *had* to go find her. Right then. Immediately. He hadn't paused to talk to Shelby any longer. He'd barely taken the time to tell his grandmother he was heading out. He'd had no thoughts other than getting to Trudy.

At the time, he'd felt annoyed. Like he had to demand to know what the hell she was thinking. He knew he'd been scowling at her when he'd ordered her to repeat what she'd said to Shelby.

He'd thought it was because he'd believed she was lying. That she'd never be able to actually say it to him. That she was just messing around.

But when she'd lifted her chin, met his gaze directly, and said, "I'm in love with you, Wyatt," his world had tilted.

And he'd realized that he'd just *needed* to hear her say it.

Because he felt the same way.

"I…" He swallowed. "I'm glad you said it."

She shook her head. "You don't have to say that."

"I do. I need you to know that. We never talked after that." He cupped her face. "Especially if you've been thinking I regret any of that."

"You…don't?"

He knew he had to be honest with her. He thought back on that night. The Community Center had been the site of a community-wide garage sale, auction, and potluck. Some people, including his grandmother, had brought homemade crafts and items like quilts, embroidered towels, wooden and metal art pieces, and even homemade candies and baked goods.

The explosion had happened toward the end of the night, when people had been cleaning up and preparing to leave. It had been an accident. There was nothing anyone could have done.

"I was messed up for a long time afterward," he finally admitted. "I did feel guilty. I did regret leaving my grandma. I thought if I'd been there, maybe she would have been outside. If I'd stayed and helped her finish cleaning up, maybe she would have already left the building. I felt selfish for bolting in the middle of helping her. But…" He focused on Trudy's face. "I know if she'd known why I was leaving, who I was with and why, she would have encouraged me to go. She would have been thrilled that we were together, Tru. She loved you. And I…" He swallowed hard. "I just couldn't stay away."

Her eyes were shiny now, and she sniffed.

Wyatt shook his head as he ran his thumb over her cheek. "My biggest regret is that I didn't talk to you after that. It was so…"

"Chaotic," she supplied. She nodded. "It was. It was a nightmare." Her fingers wrapped around his wrist. "I remember. We drove back to town, and it was crazy. And then the next day, your parents came, and you left with your mom while your dad stayed and dealt with everything. I…texted you."

He nodded. "I know. I kept that text for over a year."

Her eyes widened. "You did?"

"Yeah."

"All it said was *I loved your grandma so much.*"

"It was from you." He lifted his shoulder. "I loved the reminder that you knew her and loved her. I know she loved you too. Like I said, I think that helped me get over some of the guilt. She would have loved knowing we were out there kissing along the banks of the bayou."

Trudy gave him a smile, and he was relieved to see it seemed genuine.

"I missed you so much." He took a shaky breath. "But I couldn't come back for a long time. I felt so mixed up about everything. And then when I did come back…you weren't here."

They just looked at each other for a long moment, then she squeezed his wrist. "We're both here now."

"Yeah." He gave her a smile. "We sure as hell are. And I'm not going to be a dumbass this time."

"What's that mean?"

"It means, unlike that last summer we had, I'm going to spend as much time with you as possible, and talk to you about everything, and kiss you as much as I can."

She wet her lips. "Well, we've done a lot of talking. But there hasn't been very much kissing."

He gave her a grin. "I can fix that."

He leaned in and pressed his lips to her. But what he'd meant to be just a quick, sweet kiss, quickly turned hot. And deep. She pushed her fingers into his hair and opened her lips under his and he was lost.

They kissed for several long seconds. Maybe minutes.

A sudden boom, a burst of light, and a "whoo hoo!" from the truck next to them pulled them apart.

Trudy grinned up at him. "Fireworks."

He nodded, looking at nothing but her. "Yeah. Fireworks."

Wyatt lay back, putting his free hand behind his head, but he tugged Trudy close with his other, until she was snuggled up against his side.

They just lay quietly, watching the sparkling display above them.

But hey, he'd told her he was going to talk to her.

"So what happened with your fiancé?" he asked.

She didn't respond right away, but she took a breath and blew it out. Finally, she said, "You set the bar too high."

Wyatt looked over at her. "What?"

She kept her eyes on the sky. "My car broke down about thirty minutes from home. I called him, and he said to call the roadside assistance people. And I thought of you."

Wyatt felt his heart thump hard in his chest, but he stayed quiet.

"In his defense, I owned the car and didn't have a curfew, and that *is* what roadside assistance is for, but..." She sighed. "I thought of you. All the times you were there for me. And I realized that I wanted someone who *wanted* to be there. Who was *unreasonable* for me." She paused. Now she looked over. "Like my appendix. It made no sense for you to take me to the hospital. And for you to stay. But you did."

He nodded. "I had to."

"Yeah. I wanted that. Forever." She held his gaze for a heartbeat, then looked back to the sky. "And I realized I wasn't going to get that from him. So I broke it off."

Wyatt wasn't sure what to do with that information.

He'd indirectly been responsible for Trudy breaking off her engagement. Because of how he'd treated her, how he'd felt about her without even realizing it, ten years ago, she was single now.

He pulled her in closer and kissed the top of her head. She didn't resist. In fact, she seemed to happily cuddle closer.

And he was now lying under the stars in Autre, Louisiana for the first time in over a decade.

And he felt fucking fantastic.

HE STILL FELT FUCKING fantastic when he awoke the next morning in the bright sunshine in Autre, Louisiana.

That had a lot to do with the fact that Trudy Sinclair was wrapped around him like she was adrift in the ocean, and he was all that was keeping her afloat.

He felt fantastic when he kissed her awake.

He even felt fantastic when he realized that everyone else had already left. Quietly. Leaving him and Trudy sleeping.

There was no way his cousin, brother, and Trudy's sister hadn't noticed how they were sleeping.

But he was grinning like an idiot thinking about it.

And he even felt fantastic when they realized that Trudy's truck was stuck in the mud and when they both ended up muddy, wet, and laughing as they worked to get it out.

It was just like old times.

Except this time, he knew exactly how he felt about Trudy Sinclair, and that he was *not* letting her get away again.

"SO, I think that my problem with being in Autre all these years was definitely partly Grandma and what happened, but now I realize that it's also because Trudy wasn't here."

Wyatt rolled up another pancake and bit off half of it. It was his fourth, but *wow* these pancakes were amazing. Trudy had dropped him off at the Bed and Breakfast where Spencer and Max were staying because his bag was here in his truck, and he'd assumed he could use their room to shower and change. He would have preferred to use Trudy's shower, but that was probably going too fast.

He really wanted to go too fast with her.

"I think that being here without her just felt *wrong*," he went on, reaching for his coffee cup. "That last night in Autre was so crazy, and I don't know if I fully processed any of it. But now, seeing her again, it was like *bam!* It's all so clear. Being here without *her* has been a lot of my problem. Being with her again last night just felt *right*." He reached for a piece of bacon and bit into it. He focused on his brother. "Is that nuts?"

Spencer was sitting back in his chair, just watching Wyatt. Max was beside him, her eyes wide.

"No," Spencer said evenly. "That makes a lot of sense to me."

"Does it?" Wyatt leaned in. "Really? Because it *feels* right. But is that too fast? Can I just fall in love with her like that?" He snapped his fingers.

"It's not just like that," Spencer said. "You fell in love with her over what? Four or five years? You first met her when you were twelve or so, right?"

"I met her way before that," Wyatt said. "But that was when we started hanging out." He nodded, thinking back. "And we started really spending time just us when we were about fifteen."

"You mean, all the times you were getting in trouble together," Spencer said.

"I mean all the times I was bailing her out of trouble."

Spencer snorted. "Sure. You always pretended to be so annoyed, but you were the first one up and out when she needed something."

"She called me first," Wyatt said.

"Not in the beginning," Spencer said. "She'd call Shelby and Scott first. Or sometimes Mitch. Or even Zeke."

Wyatt frowned. Spencer was right. "Well, Shelby and Scott always acted so annoyed by being interrupted. And…"

Spencer gave him a knowing look. "You didn't want Mitch or Zeke picking her up."

"I—" But yeah. Now that he could be totally honest about how he felt about Trudy, he hadn't wanted another single, fun guy coming to her rescue.

"You were into her from the start," Spencer said.

"And you didn't want to admit it because you were afraid it would change things," Max added.

"How do you know?" Wyatt asked. "You weren't there."

Max just shrugged. "Movies, books, TV. It's classic friends-to-lovers stuff."

Wyatt took a long drink of his coffee. Then he asked, "Is it possible I've just never gotten over her?"

"Of course," Max said. "Why would you get over her? You'd just officially started something when… everything went crazy. You never had a reason to get over her. Nothing happened to break you up. You just hit pause."

"For ten years," Spencer said with an eye roll.

Wyatt frowned. "Can we just pick up from where we left off?"

Max lifted a shoulder. "Sure. Kind of. You'll have to catch up, see how much you've both changed, see if you still want the same things. Ten years is a long time. But you're both here again, she's moved back, and you live twenty minutes away. You're both single, and obviously interested. You definitely need to see where this goes."

Yeah. They did. Definitely.

Starting now. Immediately.

Wyatt pushed up out of his chair, grabbed another pancake,

and grinned at his brother and Max. "Thanks, you guys. Love you." He headed for the door but stopped and turned back. "You should try to get to know Trudy," he told Max. "She's going to be around. A lot."

CHAPTER FIVE

So she was supposed to just sit here, watch Wyatt…with his *shirt off*…run around playing sand volleyball, smiling and laughing and having a great time, and *not* become a tightly wound hot mess of emotion?

No. That wasn't happening.

She was definitely becoming a tightly wound hot mess of emotion.

Seeing him so *happy*, so free, hanging out with his family and old friends, *playing* again like they had as kids, made her want to cry. With joy. Definitely with joy.

But also with why-did-all-that-bad-bullshit-have-to-happen?

This guy—the sun-kissed, smiling, fun guy on the volleyball court—was the guy she remembered. The guy she'd fallen for.

The guy she'd missed.

And now he was also the guy who was kissing her, and sleeping with her under the stars, and acting so damned *happy* to be around her.

He'd *bounded* down the steps of the Bed and Breakfast when she'd come back to pick him up for the volleyball game. Like a damned Golden Retriever. He'd jumped up in her passenger seat, leaned over, grasped the back of her neck and hauled her in for a deep, hot, sweet kiss.

It was like all of this was happening in a dream.

But it was worse than that…

It was real. And it still might fade away tomorrow.

She didn't think he was doing it on purpose or that he would do anything intentionally to hurt her, but this was all the product of being home again, the sun, the fun, the friends on holiday, the general jovial feel around them, and him trying so fucking hard to make everything okay again.

"Okay, that's it!" Paige clapped her hands together, making Trudy jump.

She looked over at her friend, who was sitting to her right. "What?"

Paige looked past Trudy to Shelby who was sitting on her other side. Her sister nodded and scooted her lawn chair closer to Trudy's.

Paige did the same.

"Time to *spill*," Paige said. "What is going on with you and Wyatt? I go from not even knowing that you know each other to watching you be all ga-ga over one another all day, and you have yet to tell me one thing! Shelby and Mitch have filled me in on some of it, but we're *all* dying to know what's going on now."

"Have you been in touch over the past few years, and I just didn't know it?" Shelby asked, leaning forward in her chair and focusing her full attention on Trudy. "I thought you hadn't seen or heard from him in *years*. I remember that first summer he came back after his grandma died, but you stayed in Colorado that year working for that white-water rafting place. And he only stayed like a week."

Trudy opened her mouth to answer, but Paige was talking again.

"Yeah, Mitch told me everything he knows. That you and Wyatt hung out together a lot. That you were a big troublemaker, and he was always bailing you out." Paige grinned as she nudged Trudy's knee. "But that he thought Wyatt had a crush on Shelby."

Again Trudy started to respond, but Shelby flipped her hand as if to wave that all away.

"Oh, that was all just kind of joking around. I was with Scott the entire time except for like twenty-four hours that last summer before college. In fact, that's what we fought about and why we broke up for one whole day. That was the night that Wyatt came and asked me out and...." She looked at Trudy. "I told him I couldn't go out with him because Trudy was in love with him."

Paige gasped. "You *told him that*?"

"Well, yeah. I thought he should know. Because I thought he actually felt the same way," Shelby said. She looked at Trudy. "I think he thought maybe they were too good of friends to take it to the next level or something. But I also think he only asked me out because it was like a game...I was single for the first time and he had a big enough ego he just had to find out if I'd say yes, even after breaking up with a guy I'd dated for three years and was clearly madly in love with."

Paige was now leaning forward too, and the two women were talking past Trudy, *about* Trudy, as if she wasn't even there.

"But you think he actually had feelings for Trudy?" Paige asked.

"I do. And maybe he didn't even really realize it. I just remember the look on his face when I told him she'd told me she was in love with him."

Trudy frowned and looked at her sister.

"What was the look on his face?" Paige asked, her eyes wide.

"Like I'd just slapped him." Shelby grinned. "And like I'd just told him something he was *really* happy to know."

"Oh my god!" Paige said. "What did he say?"

"Where is she?" Shelby said. "That's it. Just 'where is she?'. Obviously, I knew he meant Trudy. I told him she was with some friends down by the bayou having a bonfire. He turned and stomped off without another word. He seemed mad, but...I don't think he was angry."

"What do you think he was?" Paige asked.

Shelby turned to Trudy with a sly smile. "Turned on. In love. On a mission."

Paige took a big breath and blew it out with a happy smile. "I love that." Then she looked at Trudy. "Okay, now you go. What happened when he found you?"

Trudy swallowed.

She hadn't heard Shelby's side of that story before. She'd never asked. She supposed she'd never thought it mattered.

But...maybe it did.

"Um, well, he pulled up, got out, slammed his door really hard, and just yelled, 'Trudy Sinclair get your butt up here!'

She still remembered the way her stomach had flipped. He'd sounded mad, but she hadn't been worried. For one thing, she'd never be afraid of Wyatt. For another, she'd figured the confrontation was about her sister. And if Shelby had said yes to going out with him, he wouldn't have been mad. That meant things were going Trudy's way.

"I went up the hill to meet him, and he put his hands on his hips, all belligerent, and said, 'Do you have something you want to say to me?' Trudy told them.

Her gaze went to where he was high-fiving his teammates on the volleyball court. They'd scored again. Grumpy and annoyed, or happy and having fun, that man stole her breath.

"He didn't tell you he'd been talking to Shelby or anything?" Paige asked. "He didn't say, *are you in love with me*? He wanted to hear you say it?"

Trudy looked at her friend. "I...guess?" Then it occurred to her that, yes, that was exactly what he'd wanted. "He could always tell when I was lying. I guess he wanted to *see* me say it so he could judge if it was real."

Shelby gave a little squeal. "Because he *wanted* it to be real."

"I don't know," Trudy said.

"If he *didn't*, he wouldn't have come after you," Shelby said. "He would have just let it go. Ignored it. Pretended he didn't know."

Trudy frowned. That actually made sense. Now. Ten years later.

"Well, anyway, I pretended I didn't know what he was talking about, and he tried pushing by telling me he was going to ask Shelby out. As if he hadn't already. I didn't know he had, so I was a little confused, but I told him she'd say no. He asked how I could be so sure, and I said I just knew that she would because of Scott. Then he said something like, "There's another reason, though, right?""

"Ooooh," Paige said. "He *really* wanted to hear you say it."

Yeah. He had. And Trudy actually remembered every single detail of that exchange.

"Do you have something you want to say to me?"

Trudy's heart flipped in her chest. Oh…crap…he was going to make her say it to him? Out loud? "What are you talking about?"

His eyes narrowed. "I'm going to ask your sister out."

Trudy shrugged, trying to pretend that those words weren't like him punching her in the gut. "Fine. Do it. She'll say no."

He took a step closer. "Why will she say no, Trudy?"

"Because she's in love with Scott."

"But there's something else, right?"

Trudy tipped her chin up. "What do you mean?"

His voice dropped lower. "Tell me what you said to her."

No way was she going to say those words. His ego didn't need that. "Maybe I only said it because I knew it would make her say no to you."

He took another step closer. "And why would you want her to say no to me?"

Trudy swallowed and told him a partial truth. "She and Scott belong together. I don't want you to mess it up. They'll get back together unless you get in the way."

He nodded slowly, taking another step that brought him to stand nearly on top of her. *"And why do you* really *want her to say no to me, Tru?"*

"That's it."

"I don't believe you."

She was breathing really fast. She wanted to say it. She wanted to see his reaction. "Well, that's your problem."

"Say it, Blue."

It might have been the low rumble of his voice. Or the way he was looking at her. Or the nickname. Whatever it was, finally, she lifted her chin, looked him directly in the eye, and said, "I'm in love with you, Wyatt."

Then he grasped her by the upper arms and pulled her up and into the best kiss of her life.

She'd gasped, then gone up on tiptoe, grabbed his shoulders, and kissed him back.

He'd groaned, opened his mouth, and when their tongues touched, he cupped her ass, squeezed, and then lifted her.

Her legs wrapped around him, he turned and pressed her against the side of his truck.

That kiss had only been interrupted because they'd heard the loud *boom* from the community center exploding.

They'd pulled apart, stunned by the kiss—that they'd done it *and* by how good it had been—and confused by the sound they didn't recognize. Then cell phones started ringing around the bonfire. Including theirs.

Then they'd heard the sirens.

They'd stared at each other. She still remembered the panic in his eyes. She was sure hers looked the same.

They'd answered their phones. She wasn't sure who had called him. Hers had been her father.

Without a word, Wyatt had wrapped a hand around her wrist, tugged her to the driver's side of his truck, practically thrown her inside, then climbed up after her. She hadn't argued.

In fact, they hadn't said another word to one another.

Not one.

He'd driven them back into town. They'd had to stop three blocks from the community center because of all the people and emergency vehicles. They'd sat for nearly a minute staring at the chaotic scene in front of them. Then they'd looked at each other. They'd held that stare for another almost minute.

Then they'd both gotten out and been swept up in the madness.

She'd immediately found her parents and Shelby—she and Scott were already back together—and Wyatt had disappeared into the crowd.

She hadn't seen him again until his grandmother's funeral ten days later. And then she'd only *seen* him. They hadn't spoken.

She'd texted him. Just once. He hadn't reached out. Hadn't called. Hadn't texted. She'd asked a couple of his cousins how he was, and they'd said, "Not good."

Then they'd both started their senior years of high school, and she'd tried not to think about him all the time. It had been hard. But when he hadn't come to Autre for Christmas, she'd cried. And when he hadn't come to Autre the following summer, she'd cried again. And then told herself she had to move on.

She left for college in Colorado at the end of the most depressing summer of her life, and she'd stayed there the following summer instead of returning to Autre. And the summer after that. And the one after that.

She had moved on. She'd dated. Had even been engaged. She'd finished school and started teaching. She'd had a Wyatt-free life, and she'd been happy.

But now she'd been with him again for only a few hours, and it was like *this* was how it was always supposed to be. It was like she was right back where they'd been before the explosion. She loved this boy. This man. This *person*.

He was more complicated now, certainly, but that was supposed to happen. Ten years was supposed to add layers. But she could still see her Wyatt underneath all of that.

Yes, *her* Wyatt.

Because now, ten years later, she could look back more objec-tively and see that everything he'd done for her and with her had to have meant something more than friendship.

Certainly, that last conversation had meant more. She could still conjure the look on his face. And the feel of his kiss.

There had been need there. Hope. Relief. Happiness. Hunger.

He'd wanted her declaration of love to be real. He'd wanted to hear it. He'd needed to see the truth of it for himself.

And that kiss…

God, they'd been seventeen. But that kiss had been the best of her life. Because it had been the culmination of friendship and secrets and laughter and frustration, and it had been the start of something bigger.

Or it *should have been* the start of something bigger.

She blew out a breath. "Well, fuck," she said out loud.

Paige and Shelby looked at her.

"You okay?" Paige asked.

"No." She looked at her friend, then her sister. "I'm…in love."

CHAPTER SIX

PAIGE'S EYES WIDENED, and Shelby's mouth curved into a large smile.

"Are you telling me that you've fallen in love with the guy I set you up with *yesterday*?" Paige demanded. Though she looked delighted.

It was Shelby that answered her, though. "No. She's telling you that you just happened to set her up with the guy she's always been in love with."

Trudy felt Shelby's words in her heart. In her *soul*.

Could that be true?

She looked back out to the court.

Wyatt ran at the net, jumped, and spiked the ball down onto the other team's court. JD Evans dove for it but missed it by just a centimeter.

And that was the game.

And the tournament.

Wyatt, Michael, Zeke, and Owen had won the whole thing.

The guys all rush Wyatt, piling on top of him, sand kicking up all over. Just like old times. Trudy laughed and felt the warmth rush over her. Seeing him here, seeing him happy, surrounded by people who loved him, and then seeing him immediately look for her made her heart expand, and a feeling of rightness wash through her.

Yes, it could be true that she'd always loved him and still did.

Laughing, Wyatt extricated himself and came jogging toward her. He pulled her up out of the chair, picked her up, and planted a big kiss on her lips. In front of everyone. And that felt right too.

He pulled back with a big grin, spun toward the group, and said, "See y'all later."

"No celebratory beer and swim?" Owen asked, watching them with a huge grin.

There were lots of grins, Trudy noted as she looked around. And no truly surprised expressions.

"I've had plenty of beers and swims," Wyatt said. "But I *haven't* spent enough time with Trudy rubbing all my sore muscles and telling me how hot she gets watching me play sand volleyball."

"I—what—I didn't—" Trudy started, feeling her cheeks burn.

But Wyatt just slung her over his shoulder like a sack of potatoes, scooped up her bag, where his t-shirt and sandals were tucked, and started for the parking lot.

They left the sand volleyball courts with whoops, and "be goods" and "see you kids later" called after them.

She smacked Wyatt on the butt. "I can't believe you did that."

Wow, his butt was really firm.

He just chuckled. "No one else seems surprised." He put her down next to his truck and reached past her, his sweaty, sandy body pressing against her as he unlocked the door.

"Hey," she protested weakly. "You're getting me dirty."

"Good thing we're headed for the shower then."

She wet her lips and pulled her gaze from the swirling tattoo surrounding a hawk to his face. "Okay, so you go shower at the B and B, I'll head home, and we'll meet… at Ellie's. In a couple of hours?"

He smiled and shook his head slowly. "You said you'd stick right by my side."

"Even when you…" She swallowed hard. "…shower?"

He studied her face for a moment, then lifted a hand and tugged on a strand of hair that had escaped her ponytail. "Well, I'd at least hoped you'd be in the same building."

She blew out a breath. Was she nervous about getting naked with Wyatt?

Of course she fucking was.

He was a Coast Guard. He was ripped. He probably had women throwing themselves at him all the time. A man in uniform who looked like this? Uh, yeah, Wyatt was *way* more experienced than she was.

And she liked pizza.

She loved hiking and biking and being outdoors too, which helped her keep in shape, but where Wyatt had a six-pack-almost-an-eight-pack she didn't even have a two-pack.

She was curvy, and she didn't care a bit.

Until it came to the idea of getting naked with her high school crush in a brightly lit bathroom in the middle of a sunny day.

No. Way.

He tugged her forward, making her bump into his bare six-pack with a little "Ooph," and then opened the truck's driver's side. He lifted her up, tossed her onto the seat, and then started to climb up after her.

She quickly scooted to the other side to avoid being sat on.

"I'll swing by the B and B and get my stuff, then I'll shower at your place," he said as he started the truck.

"You're inviting yourself over?" she asked, crossing her arms, mostly to keep from running her hands over his abs rather than because she was annoyed.

"Well, I figure if I take you to the B and B with me, you'll just sneak out while I'm in the shower. If we're at your place, there's a better chance you'll stick around." He pulled the truck onto the street but stopped at the stop sign and then looked over at her.

"What?" she asked. He had a point.

"Where's your house?" he asked with a grin.

"Oh. I'm… on Cherry Lane."

He chuckled. "So, only about three blocks from the bed and breakfast?"

"Yeah."

He reached over and took her hand, linking their fingers. "I'm still keepin' you right beside me."

"Why?"

"Because you got away for ten years. I don't want that to happen again. And I can practically hear those gears turning in your pretty head."

She blew out a breath. How did he know her this well? Had they really been that close all those years ago? But yeah… they had.

He'd always known when she was scheming. More than once he'd showed up before she'd even needed to call for help. He'd followed her after watching her body language or reading into something she said. He also always knew when she was lying or had done something she was trying to cover up. He'd once thrown her over his shoulder, just like he had at the volleyball court, stomped down to the docks, and thrown her in the bayou, refusing to let her out until she confessed.

"This is all just crazy. And fast. And not at all what I was expecting this weekend. And…"

"You're worried it's not real."

She looked over at him, butterflies fluttering in her stomach. "Well, yeah." She and Wyatt had always been honest with each other. "I think that you're trying really hard to make this weekend fun and make good memories to replace bad ones, and that's awesome. I'm fully supportive of that. Happy to be a part of it. I love that you're back and having a great time with every-one. But I also think that maybe you're building some of this—"

She motioned with her finger between them. "—up into something more than it is to add to those good feelings and to maybe cover up some of the bad stuff that's still lurking."

He didn't say anything for a few seconds. Then he nodded. "That's okay." He ran his thumb over the back of her knuckles.

"What is?"

"To not be sure of this thing between us yet. I've waited ten years to have you back. I'll take as much time as you need to prove it's real."

Her heart flipped, her stomach swooped, and her panties got a little wet.

His confidence was unflagging.

And truthfully…that's what she'd wanted to hear. Even if this seemed fast and hard to believe that it could still be real. That the timing was actually great. That this chance to make new memories was also the perfect chance for them to start over. Or pick up where they'd left off.

There was no way she was going to be able to avoid this.

The Wyatt showering in her house thing…at least without joining him.

And the being in love with him.

It was crazy. It was maybe stupid. But she was going to do this.

They pulled up in front of her house, and Wyatt started to get out, but her hand flew out, gripping his forearm. He turned back, question in his eyes.

"I was in love with you," she blurted.

His eyebrows arched. "Tru—"

"I just need you to know that. It wasn't just because of Shelby. I told her about it *that* night because I wanted her to say no to you. And yes, a little because of Scott. And because I didn't want you to get hurt and all of that. But…" Trudy sucked in a breath. "I don't think you would have been hurt." She realized it as she said it out loud. "You and Shelby might have gone out a couple of times, but you would have just had some fun and realized you would just be friends. She would have still gotten back with Scott. He would have always taken her back. You couldn't have ruined them. And you wouldn't have been broken-hearted because you never would have actually fallen in love with her." She frowned as all of the realizations hit her consciousness for the first time. "I think I knew all of that deep down, even then."

Trudy met Wyatt's eyes. He was watching her intently.

"So...it was true," she said softly. "I was in love with you. And if it wasn't that night, I would have told my sister eventually anyway. Like when you did actually get serious with someone else or when you left at the end of that summer, and she wanted to know why I was crying my eyes out." She stopped, breathed again, and shrugged. "So yeah, you should know that. My feelings, what I said…that was real."

He waited for a second, making sure she was done. Then he nodded. "Okay. That's really good to know."

"It is?" Was he going to say it back? Was he going to tell her how he felt about her back then?

"Yeah. It's going to make this next part even better." He gave her a slow grin that made heat twirl through her chest and belly. "And it was going to be pretty fucking good anyway."

"This…" She stopped and wet her suddenly very dry lips. "Next part?"

"Yeah."

He got out of the truck, slammed the door, and rounded the front as she struggled to make her own hand follow the command to open her door.

He was at her door, pulling it open a moment later. He reached for her hips, pulling her to the edge of the seat. He stepped between her knees.

"The part where I tell you that if we'd had even thirty more seconds to talk that night, without the fucking world ending around us, I would have told you that I was in love with you too." He pulled her off the truck seat.

Thank God.

Trudy hadn't realized how much she'd wanted, *needed*, to hear that.

She automatically wrapped her legs around his waist and her arms around his neck. She wasn't sure she was breathing. But her heart was sure as hell pounding, so at least she was still alive. For now.

Then he added, "And then the part where I take you upstairs, strip you naked, carry you into the shower, and finally make you mine."

That was when her heart stopped.

Wyatt turned and started toward her front door, carrying her.

Trudy wasn't sure what to do. Or feel. Or say. Or *do*. So she just went with her instinct. She buried her face in his neck and just hung on.

CHAPTER SEVEN

Ten years was not fast.

Actually, he and Trudy had been falling in love for more like fourteen years.

Okay, they'd fallen in love over the course of the four years of knowing each other, getting into trouble together, getting out of trouble together, sharing secrets, and knowing each other better than anyone else knew them.

Then, they'd gone their separate ways, done their own things, developed into who they were today over the next ten years. They'd grown up. Tried new things. Learned about themselves, the world, what was important to them, what they cared about.

And what they'd figured out had brought them both back to Autre ten years later. At the same time.

Trudy was here, to live and teach and be a part of this community again.

Wyatt was here to recapture the things that were important to him that he'd lost and wanted back—friendships, family, his sense of roots and personal history, and the comfort that came from that.

It was actually no surprise to him, when he thought about all of that, that he and Trudy would both be here now, ten years later, older, better in some ways, but still looking for something. And then, in the course of just a few hours, realizing that they'd found the rest of what they needed in each other.

A little crazy? Maybe. Sappy? For sure. But real? Absolutely.

And he didn't have to put a ring on her finger today. But he did have to convince her that he wasn't letting her go again.

Wyatt let her down in front of her door, but he backed her up against it, took her face in his hands, and kissed her deeply.

She leaned into him, wanting to be as close as he did. Her fingers were in his hair, and her mouth opened under his immediately.

He swept his tongue against hers, gripping her hips and pressing into her, letting her feel how hard he was, how affected he was, and how much he wanted her.

He wouldn't push her, but if she didn't stop him, he was going to take everything she'd give him.

She gave a sweet little combination moan-gasp, and he dragged his mouth along her jaw and down her throat. "I'm getting you even dirtier now," he said gruffly.

"I hope this is just the start of that," she said.

Fuck, yes. He lifted his head and looked her directly in the eye. "How dirty do you want to be with me, Tru?"

"I have a feeling you can make me dirtier than I've ever been." She paused. "And I want *that*."

His whole body tightened, and his cock throbbed. "I want to make you absolutely filthy."

Her fingers tightened in his hair.

"You'll have to let me know if I'm going too far or too fast. Talk to me, and I promise you, this will be really good for us both."

She laughed lightly. "Wyatt, I'm not worried about that at all. I trust you. And I've wanted you since I was fifteen years old."

He squeezed her hips. "Okay, then promise to talk to me because I want to hear all kinds of delicious dirty things from this sweet mouth." His eyes went from hers to her mouth, and he watched as she licked her bottom lip.

"Okay," she said softly. "I'm, um…my bathroom gets a lot of sunlight, and I'm a little nervous about being totally naked in front of you in broad daylight."

His eyes widened. "Tru, you have *absolutely* nothing to worry about. I'm dying to see you." He squeezed her hips again, then ran his hands around to her ass, pulling her against him again. "Do you feel what you do to me? I can't wait to worship every inch of you. I've seen you in bikinis and shorts, and I believe I saw your bare ass one time skinny dipping if I'm not mistaken."

He wasn't mistaken.

She smiled but shook her head. "Yeah, ten years ago. When my metabolism was a lot faster, and I was a teenager."

"Yeah. And you were kind of scrawny." He palmed her ass with both hands. "Now you're a woman. With all kinds of delicious curves. Places to hold on, places to really sink in, with no worries about going too hard." He pressed against her.

He heard her little intake of air, and her pupils dilated.

"I'm not a kid anymore either," he told her, dipping his head to put his nose against hers. "I'm a man. And I like to fuck *women*. And you, Tru, are all woman." He dragged his mouth along her jaw, abrading her skin with his stubble, until he got to her ear. "Let me at these curves, Blue. It's going to be so good that you have a little padding for the things I have planned."

She half-moaned, half-laughed. "Oh, my God." She pushed him back slightly and looked up at him. She was clearly amused, but there was a hint of mischief in her eyes.

"What?" he asked when she didn't say anything.

"I was just thinking that I should be surprised you're so sexy and kind of a dirty talker, but I'm not. It fits. You were always very willing to get in trouble with me. You liked to pretend that you were the hero, the one bailing me out and covering for me and supposedly keeping things from getting worse, but you never actually stopped me from doing anything. And now that

I'm thinking about it more, I don't think you minded all those times I landed on you or you had to pick me up or put your hands on my ass."

Looking down into the eyes that were so familiar and yet held a fun, new, I-want-to-know-all-your-stories-and-secrets edge, Wyatt nodded, "I think you're right. I maybe didn't even admit it to myself then, but the reason I was always so willing to show up for you was because I was falling head over heels. And because you were always a hell of a good time."

Her smile now had a touch of true affection in it. "I hope I can keep you interested now without all that excitement."

But he didn't even have to think about his response. "When I think back, do you know the times that first come to mind?"

"The standing waist-deep in the bayou pushing on a car that just kept sinking lower and noticing the gator slipping into the water off the shore about twenty feet away?" she asked. "Or swiping three jars of moonshine from Leo's stash and then dropping one on the concrete and having it break open with the *loudest* crash I swear I've ever heard, running for the trees, and hiding for *two hours* because he'd just dragged a chair out there and sat by the broken jar waiting to see who came back to try to clean it up? Or the time *we* caught Zeke and Zander swiping moonshine, and we followed them to the abandoned bayou cabin thinking we'd blackmail them, and they tied us up and left us there? Or the time we picked up that hitchhiker and drove her to Houston, and then she stole my purse, and we had to call Owen for a ride home when we ran out of gas and had no money, *and* we had to go to New Orleans the next day and replace my credit card, and birth control pills?"

Wyatt was chuckling by the time she finished, but he shook his head. "Actually, no. The ones that come to mind first are us making peanut butter and jelly sandwiches in my grandma's kitchen at two a.m. after we got home late from…whichever adventure."

"We did that more than once," she said softly.

"Yep. And I liked that part because we just talked. And things were really normal. We talked about normal stuff. How much you hated chemistry class and how much I loved baseball and stories about our families and that we both wanted to have houses big enough to have all of our kids' cousins sleep over all the time when we grew up."

She was watching him intently now.

He lifted a hand and brushed her hair back. "I think of you whenever I eat peanut butter and jelly."

"I still want a big house like that for that reason," she said.

"Me, too."

And he couldn't not kiss her any longer.

He dipped his head, but she met him halfway.

The kiss was hungry and deep but slower. As he kissed her, holding her face in both hands, he felt her reach behind her and twist the knob on the door, then push it open.

No one locked their doors in Autre. At least not while they were in town and going in and out during the day.

They stumbled across the threshold, and Wyatt kicked the door shut behind them. Then he was tugging her dress up and over her head and tossing it to the side. He lifted his head only long enough to get her dress past her lips. Then he was kissing her again.

He was still shirtless, so he worked on kicking his shoes off as she did the same.

He pulled away to shed his socks. And to take her in.

She was in a simple bra and panty set, but he had to smile. This dress was blue, her bra was white, and her panties were red.

"How very patriotic of you, Ms. Sinclair," he said.

She dipped her head. "Thank you."

"And just who did you think was going to be appreciating your holiday flair here?" he asked, pulling her against him again.

"Honestly, I did it for myself because I thought it was funny," she said. "But…I'm not mad about honoring an active serviceman this way." She ran her hands up his sides and over his chest.

His body heated and tightened. "You feel like showing me some appreciation, huh?"

She ran her hands from his chest, across his shoulders, and down over his biceps. Her eyes followed her hands. They'd been up close before. They'd touched each other before, but it had never been like this. It had never been sexual. But with her hands and eyes on him now, it felt so strangely familiar. Maybe she hadn't touched him this way before, but she was *meant* to. And he needed more of it.

"I would love to *appreciate* you in a lot of ways," she murmured, stroking her hands over his forearms and looking up at him through her lashes.

Yep. He needed *a lot* more.

He bent and swept her up into his arms. "Where's the shower?"

She laughed and pointed at the stairs to his right. "Upstairs. Through my bedroom. Third door on the right."

He carried her up the stairs and down the hall, through her room—they'd come back to the big four-poster bed eventually—and into her master bathroom. The house was an older, two-story but the bathroom looked like it had been remodeled and updated in the past few years. There was a tub that sat across from the vanity, separate from the walk-in, all-glass shower straight ahead.

Wyatt didn't put Trudy down until they were inside the shower. He blocked her with his body as he turned the shower on and adjusted the temperature. Then with the water cascading down his back, he faced her.

"You good?" he asked.

She shook her head, and his heart thumped hard.

"We're both overdressed, and I really need your hands on me," she said, stepping forward.

His breath rushed out of his lungs. Thank God. "Okay, let's

lay this out," he said. "I'm going to soap up and wash off over here." He pointed at the spot where he was standing in the shower. "You're going to keep your sweet ass over there for a minute." He pointed to where she was standing. "Because when we start touching each other, it's not going to stop even long enough for soap."

Her grin was bright and clearly pleased and a touch sly. "Okay."

He hooked his thumbs in the top of his shorts. He paused and focused on her face. Her eyes were pinned on the bulge behind the thin material. He grinned. "You ready?"

She laughed. "Yes. Let's go. Let's see if you have reason to be so full of yourself."

He chuckled. "I'm not the only one who's going to be full of me."

Her mouth dropped open. As she recovered from his comment, he stripped his shorts and underwear off. Then her mouth dropped open again as she took him in for the first time.

Just having her eyes on him made him need to wrap a hand around his cock and squeeze to ease some of the ache. "Blue," he said gruffly. He wasn't sure what he intended with that except to pull her eyes to his and off his painfully hard dick.

She looked up at him. "Yeah?"

"You okay?"

"Better all the time."

He huffed out a laugh. "How about you take some clothes off?"

Her bra was white, and even with him blocking the water, she was getting wet, and that bra was becoming more and more transparent.

She reached behind her back and unhooked the bra, peeling it away.

Her breasts were perfect. Fucking perfect. He had to squeeze his cock again as it pulsed with need. Her nipples were tight on the sweet, full mounds, and his mouth watered with the temptation to get them against his tongue.

He took an involuntary step forward, but she held up a hand. "Soap."

He groaned. "What was I thinking bringing you in here with me?"

"That it was going to be a really great new adventure for us," she said with a smile that was full of I've-got-you-right-where-I-want-you.

And she was right. This was an exciting place they hadn't been together before, and he couldn't wait. He stroked himself again.

Then she pushed her panties to the floor and stepped out of them.

And he forgot how to breathe.

Trudy kicked her panties to the side. She reached up, cupping her breasts. "Wy?"

"Y—" He cleared his throat. "Yeah?" Somehow he pulled his eyes from her gorgeous body to her face.

"Soap."

He sucked in air. "Right."

He blindly reached for the rack where her bottles of shampoo and other items were held. But he fumbled around, not finding a bar of soap.

She stepped close and reached past him. Her breasts brushed his chest, and he groaned. *"Blue."*

"Here." She picked up a bottle, then took one of his hands, turning it palm up, flipped the top of the bottle, and poured body wash into his hand. She pressed his palm against his chest. "Wash."

She grinned up at him, clearly enjoying how she was affecting him.

He began circling his hand over his pec, and she started to step back, but he grabbed her wrist with his free hand and kept her from stepping back. "Nope. You're staying here."

"You said I was supposed to stay over there." She jabbed her thumb over her shoulder.

"Changed my mind." He took the bottle of wash from her, turned *her* hand palm up, and poured body wash into it. Then he put her hand on his chest. "Help me. It will go faster."

She stroked her hand over him. Slowly. "You sure about that?"

He dipped his head, looking into her eyes. "The faster I get washed, the sooner I can get my mouth between your legs."

Her hand froze for two seconds. Then she started scrubbing. Quickly.

He laughed, and together they washed him. Head to toe. But he had to keep moving her hands off his abs and lower, reminding her to move over his back, shoulders, neck, and other less tempting places. She lingered over his ass. But then, finally, she wrapped her hands around his cock, and he couldn't move her. Not for anything.

She stroked him as he stepped back under the spray to rinse off.

Then he was clean. And more than ready for what was next.

He shut off the shower, then picked her up. She wrapped her legs around his waist, his cock nestling against the soft, wet heat he couldn't wait to get more personal with.

He strode into the bedroom and tossed her onto the bed.

"You're going to get everything all wet," she protested.

"I hope there are some things that are already all wet," he teased. But he pulled the duvet off the bed entirely, throwing it to the floor.

She giggled and scooted up the bed toward the headboard. "But my *sheets* are going to get all wet and be uncomfortable to nap on after."

He climbed up, crawling after her. "I promise you won't care about anything but my tongue in about two minutes," he told her. But he grabbed one ankle and pulled her to the edge of the bed.

Her gorgeous breasts bounced, and he got a very nice view of the pussy he didn't even know he'd been craving all his life until today. But man, he knew it now.

"But I have an idea," he told her.

He flipped her to her stomach, then pulled her hips off the bed, bending her over the edge. Only her upper body was supported on the mattress now. She gasped as he ran a big hand up her back. She straightened her arms, arching her back, her hair falling forward.

Fuck, that was sexy as hell.

He gathered her hair in one hand and kissed the back of her neck.

"We'll nap, cuddled up close, on the other side," he told her. "And by the time I'm done with this next part, we'll be mostly air-dried."

"Next part?" she asked, breathless.

"The making you scream my name with just my mouth part," he told her, using his knee to spread her legs and running a hand up her inner thigh.

She shivered, and he knew it was not because she was cold.

He leaned over her, taking both breasts in his hands, teasing her nipples, and putting his mouth against her ear to growl, "Then I can flip you over and spread you out so I can see your pretty eyes when I fuck you nice and deep for the first time."

"*Wyatt*," she moaned, pressing back into him, her ass against his cock.

"Oh yeah, Blue, it's all me, honey. All. Me." He gripped her hips and sank to his knees behind her. He ran his hand up her inner thigh again, taking in the sight of all the delicious pink between her legs, wet and glistening for him. "Damn, this is a gorgeous sight." He cupped her, feeling how hot she was.

She rubbed against his hand, and he felt his cock pulse. She needed him and was willing to seek out the friction and pressure she wanted.

He curled a finger, sinking in to his first knuckle. "Jesus, Blue, you're so damned tight and hot."

"Yes," she whispered. "More."

"There's so much more," he promised. "Everything you need." He pulled his finger out and circled over her clit, and she moved closer, seeing more pressure. "Tell me what you want, honey."

"You, Wyatt," she panted. "Please. Fill me up."

Damn. He reached down and stroked himself as he slid a finger deep, then added a second. "Like that?"

She pressed back. "Yes. More."

He moved his fingers in and out, gritting his teeth at how fucking good even that felt. He wasn't going to last long inside her, and he had to make this good for her. This had to be the best she'd ever had because it was going to be for him. She was it. All he'd ever want or need.

He lifted her, turned them both quickly so he was leaning against the bed, and then put her feet on either side of his thighs.

"Come here," he growled, his hands on her hips, positioning her. He lifted one of her knees up onto the mattress and shifted his body until he was perfectly positioned for her to sit on his face. "Grab that bedpost and hang on tight Blue."

"Wyatt!" She gasped as he gripped her hips and gave her pussy a long lick.

He circled her clit with the tip of his tongue, then sucked, and she just cried out an, "Oh my God!"

She was indeed holding onto the bedpost with one hand, but the other was gripping his hair. Hard.

He didn't care. He licked, and sucked, and fucked her with his tongue and fingers, unrelenting as her gasps, and cries, and words—"Wyatt! Yes! Oh yes! More! Please!"—told him just what to do.

In only a few minutes, she climbed to the peak and flew right off the edge, pulling his hair and calling his name.

Fuck yes, she was calling his name.

She had in the past. She'd called out when she'd needed help, when she'd been laughing so hard she couldn't say anything else when she was excited to show or tell him something. But never like this. *This* was the one he'd been waiting for. The one he'd needed most.

Her body was still rippling with pleasure when he grasped her around the waist and set her back so he could get to his feet. He cupped her face, kissing her hungrily, making her taste herself on his tongue and lips. Then he turned her and again tossed her onto the bed.

"There's one part of you that's still dripping wet," he said as he put a knee on the mattress between her legs, his eyes on the perfect pussy he'd only begun to worship. "But the rest of you is dry enough for the bed, right?"

She was still breathing a little hard, but she nodded.

"Good." He climbed fully up onto the bed between her legs.

Trudy was propped up on her elbows, watching him. He fisted his cock, loving the way her eyes followed the action of him stroking himself, and her breathing sped up again.

"Where are your condoms, Blue?"

Her eyes flew to his face. "What? You don't have any?"

He frowned. "No. Not with me. I was playing sand volleyball."

"You didn't put any in your bag when you packed to come over here?"

"I didn't even bring any to Autre with me," he told her. "I had no plans on having sex this weekend."

Her eyes widened. "You…this isn't… don't you just…"

He lifted a brow. "No, I don't hook up every weekend, and I don't carry condoms everywhere I go."

She slumped back onto the pillows behind her. "Well, I don't have any!"

He frowned. "You don't? What the hell? You don't use condoms when you sleep with the guys you meet online dating or whatever?"

She sighed. "I haven't slept with *anyone* since I moved back to Autre. Actually, for months before that." Her cheeks got pink, but she met his eyes when she said, "I've actually only slept with two guys. Before you. Before this."

He stared at her. He fucking loved that. Way more than he should. He knew that her adventurous and rules-are-for-suckers attitude from high school didn't automatically mean that she'd be adventurous when it came to sex, but he wouldn't have been surprised to find that she had found sex a lot of fun and had explored it fully.

But to find out she *hadn't* made a caveman part of him very happy.

"You really like that, don't you?" she asked, reading him as clearly as she always had.

He grinned. "Yeah."

She rolled her eyes, but she was smiling. "Well, it's very inconvenient right now, considering it means I don't have condoms." She pulled her bottom lip between her teeth.

"I'll go get some." Wyatt started to push back off the bed. "This *is* happening. Don't move. Don't cover up. Don't…" He studied her. Her lips were pink and puffy from his kisses, her hair was coming loose, her body was flushed and so fucking gorgeous, all spread out naked, and she looked…happy. Okay, a little frustrated about the condom situation. But happy. "Just don't move. Stay just like this."

"Actually…"

He stopped from reaching for his bag.

"I'm on the pill. And I haven't had sex in a long time. I've had a physical since the last time, and I'm negative for…all the things."

His heart thudded hard in his chest. "Me too," he said.

"Then… you don't really have to go get any."

If the idea of her not having much experience and only two lovers before him had made him feel like a caveman, the idea of fucking her bare made him actually growl.

He crawled back up on the bed. He leaned in until their noses nearly touched. "I've never fucked anyone without a condom."

"Oh, well, if you don't want—"

He kissed her hungrily, his hands roaming all over her body. He plucked, then pinched her nipples, then dropped his mouth to first one, then the other, sucking them into hard, sensitive points.

"Wyatt!" she gasped.

"I fucking want. I want so damned much. If you're okay with it, I will gladly take you bare." He lifted his head. "You're it, Blue. You're my last."

Her eyes widened, and her lips parted, but before she could say anything, he slid his hand down over her body and between her legs. He cupped her.

"And this is mine. Once we do this, once I have you, I won't be able to let you go."

She moaned, and her legs shifted restlessly on the bed. "Wyatt."

"Say yes. Say that's what you want. Say you're mine."

She arched against his hand, but her eyes were firmly on his when she said the most beautiful, hot, devastating thing he'd ever heard.

"I've always been yours, Wyatt."

CHAPTER EIGHT

IF SHE WAS DREAMING, she was going to kill whoever came along and woke her up.

Wyatt Landry was not just naked in her bed. He had not just made her come harder than she'd ever come before. But now he was *claiming her*? In the hottest, sexiest way she could imagine.

"Say you're mine." His voice was gruff, his eyes were swirling with emotion, and she felt like her heart was going to burst in her chest.

"I've always been yours, Wyatt." It was the truth. It was how she felt to her very soul.

It was crazy. It felt fast. She had awakened yesterday, not having seen in him a decade. And now she was in his arms, and they were talking like this was forever.

And it felt *right*.

His mouth crashed down on hers, and he moved over her, his cock heavy and hard against her, and she *had* to have him inside her. Right. Now.

She shifted her legs, bent one knee, and tipped her pelvis. Then she reached between them, gave him a long stroke, then lined him up with her center.

"In case it wasn't *very* clear," he said roughly against her mouth. "I loved you that night too. And I know now that I've never stopped."

She felt tears pricking the backs of her eyes. "I do know."

And she did.

She hadn't. If someone had asked her while she was having her first cup of coffee yesterday if Wyatt Landry loved her, she would have laughed. If someone had asked her on the way to the fireworks last night if Wyatt Landry had been as crazy about her in high school as she had been about him, she would have said no way.

But now… just hours later…she knew.

It had always been him.

"Thank you," he said, looking into her eyes.

"Thank you?" She smiled up at him, confused. "For what?"

"For not giving this heart away to anyone else."

That heart completely melted. "How could I?" she asked, her throat feeling tight as if she might cry. "You had it with you wherever you were."

He sucked in a long, deep breath. Then he kissed her again, deeply. When he lifted his head, he said gruffly, "Need you."

"Yes. *Please.*"

He thrust forward, filling her up, the stretch delicious. Her entire body lit on fire, and she gasped his name.

"Fuck. Blue. Baby. You feel so good."

She lifted her hips. "Yes. God. Yes."

"I can't… I want to…"

"Do. It." She didn't even know what exactly he wanted to do, but she *wanted* it.

"Fuck," he muttered. Then he put a hand under her ass, lifted her, and thrust again. Hard and deep.

Then again.

It was so, so good.

"God, I'm never letting you out of this bed," he said.

She never wanted out. "More, Wyatt. Harder."

"Oh fuck." He looked at her for a moment, then apparently came to some important decision. He reached under one thigh, lifted her leg, and propped it on his shoulder.

When he thrust in again, it was so, so deep.

"God, *yes!*"

"Yes. That's my girl," he praised. "Fuck, you're so good. You can take all of me, can't you, Blue? Anything I've got?"

"Yes. Yes, please." She didn't even really know what she was agreeing to. But if Wyatt wanted to do it to her, she was in.

He thrust deep a few more times, and then he picked up the pace.

He was fucking her hard now, the headboard bouncing against the wall, and Trudy could feel every single thrust throughout her entire body.

This was…heaven. This was how it was supposed to feel. She wanted to feel owned, claimed, like she was *his*. She wanted every part of her body affected by his.

He reached between them, moving his body so the leg on his shoulder spread wider, and he circled her clit as he said, "Come apart for me, Blue. Milk my cock. Give it all up for me. Be mine."

And that was it. Her body went up and over the glorious cliff, her orgasm shooting through her before she even really felt it coming on.

"Wyatt! Yes! Oh, yes! Yes, yes, yes!"

"*Fuck*," he pushed out between gritted teeth.

As she started to come down, he gripped both of her hips and pounded into her, stroking deep, and then she felt him tense.

"Blue, yes. God, yes."

They lay spent, sprawled across her bed for nearly ten minutes after, neither of them moving. Or speaking. They just breathed. And touched. Their legs were tangled, her fingers were in his hair, his hand rested possessively on her belly.

And she let the pleasure roll over her. Not just the physical pleasure but the realization that *this* was real. Fully.

Finally.

"Hey, Blue?" Wyatt said five minutes later after he'd caught his breath.

"Yeah?"

"I meant it when I said that I was willing to take all the time you need, to take this slow, to get to know each other again and not push to go too fast by wanting to see you every day, and asking you if you want to move in together in like a month, and proposing after only dating for a couple of months."

Her breath lodged in her chest, and she forced herself to lie very still and just say, "Okay."

He rolled toward her. "But I want to take it all back."

Her heart thudded hard, and she had a hard time swallowing.

"I'm basically on the verge of proposing right now," he said.

She looked over at him. Her sweet, loving, sexy, dirty-talking Golden Retriever Coast Guard, who she'd fallen in love with at age sixteen. God, she wanted him to propose.

They were both crazy.

"No kidding," she said, nonchalantly.

"You're not surprised?"

Trudy felt a laugh bubble up. She rolled toward him. "Do you know the *first* time I realized that you're slightly bananas—in a good way—and will do anything for me?"

"When I climbed up in Jeremy Hunter's tree house to spy on his parents' barbecue because you were sure they were going to discuss how the PTA was conspiring to oust Principal Morris?"

She grinned. "You did that because it kept *me* from doing it, and you were so worried about what would happen if I got caught." She wiggled closer and kissed him. "That was so sweet and protective. But no."

"When I told Owen that I was the one that dented his truck?"

She got even closer and kissed him again. "That was also sweet and protective. But no."

"When I hid those two stray kittens in my closet for a week until you could find them a home?"

She was pressed against him completely now, and she wrapped her arms around his neck. She put her lips against his and said, "Also sweet and protective…of them…but no."

Wyatt's hands went to her ass. "Okay, when?"

"When we were thirteen, and you gave me your whole double bacon cheeseburger *and* your strawberry milkshake when I told you I hadn't had breakfast or lunch that day." She kissed him. "In fact, you *insisted* I eat it." She kissed him again.

His hands dropped to her ass, and he pulled her up and over to straddle him. "That is *very* interesting information, Ms. Sinclair."

"It is?" She grinned down at him. "Why's that?"

"Because that day, watching you eat that burger and drink my milkshake without a single bit of hesitation—or really even taking a breath—was when I decided that you were not like the other girls I knew, that hanging out with you might be not so bad, and that I liked taking care of you."

She laughed and ground down against his hardening cock. "Not so bad huh? And now, what do you think?"

He squeezed her hips and gave her a big grin that was full of love…and promise.

"That I am *definitely* going to propose to you."

Her heart flipped. "It's not too soon?"

"Blue, I'm super pissed about all the secrets, and adventures, and kittens, and burgers we've missed over the past ten years."

"Well…before you get down on one knee…"

He lifted a brow.

"Can I maybe get down on *both* of mine?"

She circled her hips, and he gave a low growl.

The next thing she knew, he'd flipped her over and was behind her. "Hands *and* knees, Blue."

"We're going to be late for the barbecue."

He ran a hand over her ass. "We sure are. But everyone should probably get used to that. It's going to be happening a lot. For the rest of our lives."

AND NOT ONE single person was surprised that they arrived two hours late and completely forgot to bring anything to the potluck.

Nor were they surprised that Wyatt spent that night in Autre.

And the next one.

And the next one.

Thank you so much for reading Red, White, & Bayou! I hope you enjoyed Wyatt and Trudy's story!

Up next is **Always Bayou,** Beau and Becca's story!
They grew up next door to one another.
Not exactly friends.
Not really enemies.
But definitely not crushes or lovers.

Until...they were.

∽

Find all of my books at
ErinNicholas.com
including a printable book list!

And join in on all the FAN FUN!

Join my **email list!**
bit.ly/Keep-In-Touch-Erin
(be sure you get those dashes and capital letters in there!)

And be the first to hear about my news, sales, freebies, behind-the-scenes, and more!

Or for even more fun, join my **Super Fan page** on Facebook and chat with me and other super fans every day! Just search Facebook for Erin Nicholas Super Fans!

MORE FROM ERIN'S BAYOU WORLD!

Want more from my bayou world? I've got so much more sexy fun for you!

Boys of the Bayou
My Best Friend's Mardi Gras Wedding (Josh & Tori)
Sweet Home Louisiana (Owen & Maddie)
Beauty and the Bayou (Sawyer & Juliet)
Crazy Rich Cajuns (Bennett & Kennedy)
Must Love Alligators (Chase & Bailey)
Four Weddings and a Swamp Boat Tour (Mitch & Paige)

*

Boys of the Bayou Gone Wild
Otterly Irresistible (Charlie& Griffin)
Heavy Petting (Fletcher & Jordan)
Flipping Love You (Zeke & Jill)
Sealed With a Kiss (Donovan & Naomi)
Say It Like You Mane It (Zander & Caroline)
Head Over Hooves (Drew & Rory)
Kiss My Giraffe (Knox & Fiona)
Better Safe Than Safari (Colin & Hayden)

*

Bayou Blades
Merry Mayhem (JD & Thea)
Just Don't Call It Love (Alex & Nora)

*

Bad Boys of the Bayou
The Best Bad Boy (Jase & Priscilla)
Bad Medicine (Nick & Brooke)
Bad Influence (Marc & Sabrina)
Bad Taste In Men (Luke & Bailey)
Not Such a Bad Guy (Reagan & Christopher)
Return of the Bad Boy (Jackson & Annabelle)
Bad Behavior (Carter & Lacey)
Got It Bad (Nolan & Randi)

*

Boys of the Big Easy
Easy Going prequel novella (Gabe & Addison)
Going Down Easy (Gabe & Addison)
Taking It Easy (Logan & Dana)
Eggnog Makes Her Easy (Matt & Lindsey)
Nice and Easy (Caleb & Lexi)
Getting Off Easy (James & Harper)

❦

And much more—
including my printable booklist— at
ErinNicholas.com

ABOUT ERIN NICHOLAS

Lover of coffee, cats, cookies, and other c-words (also tacos) **Erin
Nicholas is the NYT and USA
Today bestselling author** of over sixty romances.

If you want to have a latte, and chat about all things
New Orleans, anything Schitt's Creek, or socializing stray cats,
she's your girl. And, of course, if you
love rom coms with swoony heroes who fall hard, amazing
found families, and quirky small towns.
She lives in the middle of the US with her husband and too
many cats (his opinion, not hers).

Find her and all her books at
www.ErinNicholas.com

**And find her on Facebook, BookBub, Goodreads, and
Instagram!**

Editor: Lindsey Faber

Cover design: Beck and Dot Book Cover Design

Paperback ISBN: 978-1-967534-17-3